D0116321

Foreword

On a first encounter you might say that only a mother could love a Wolf-eel.

Wrong! Any child that reads Jacqui Stanley's story, *Wolfie the Wolf-eel*, will welcome this marine denizen into the pantheon of undersea adorables.

If you have never seen a Wolf-eel yourself, you will not know that it will appear to be one of the least likely marine animals that you would clothe in a delightful, child-like, warm, vulnerable and ready-to-love personality. With a face like Statler and Waldorf's in the *Muppet Show*, a prognathian jaw like an English bulldog's and canines as formidable as a hippo's, a Wolf-eel can be daunting at a diver's first encounter.

Jacqui Stanley is a skilled writer with an abundance of whimsical fancy. She is also a seasoned scuba diver doughty enough to dive the frigid waters of the Gulf Islands between the east coast of Vancouver Island and the mainland of British Columbia. Those dark waters are the home of the Wolf-eel and the largest octopuses in the world. Thus, her charming story is grounded in real contact with Wolf-eels and many hours of watching the behavior of their families. She has stroked them. She has fed them sea urchins. She has become their friend. She knows them well.

It is this real experience factor that imbues the story with a base of accurate behavior around which she can appealingly weave her tale. In my childhood I loved the Uncle Wiggily stories. I am still delighted with writing that can give animals human characteristics and reach across a child's imagination with enough appeal in the style and an easy plot to hold the young reader's interest. The transition from aquarium to freedom in the marine environment nicely touches on one of the many environmental activities well-managed aquaria are involved in today. I also liked Jacqui's viewpoint from the young Wolf-eels as they observed the strange animals on the other side of the glass wall. The perception by children of intelligence and sophisticated social patterns in animals they read about and observe is a growth that I hoped to foster in my own children when we all dove together in Tahiti years ago.

The late E.B. White, creator of *Charlotte's Web* and *Stuart Little*, would have loved *Wolfie the Wolf-eel*, I know. When we lived in Maine, he was a dear friend. Back in New Jersey, we corresponded from time to time. In answer to my letter mentioning that I was thinking of writing, he said he was dismayed to hear it. He pointed out that "A writer can go for days — and even weeks — without ever seeing a moray eel." So, too, might another miss out on Wolf-eels. I think he would have been delighted with Jacqui Stanley, not only a real friend of Wolf-eels, but also an accomplished, skillful writer who has turned out a most commendable and enjoyable children's story about these creatures.

Stan Waterman

"The Man Who Loves Sharks"

LIFE CYCLE OF THE WOLF-EEL
Anarrhichthys ocellatus

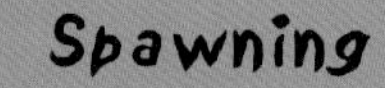

Spawning

Wolf-eel parents spawn every winter wrapping themselves around the egg mass to protect it

Choosing a Mate

They will stay together for the rest of their lives, which can last for decades.

Sedentary Mature Adult

At this stage the Wolf-eel is three or four years old. It will find a mate and settle in a den along a rocky shoreline or on a reef.

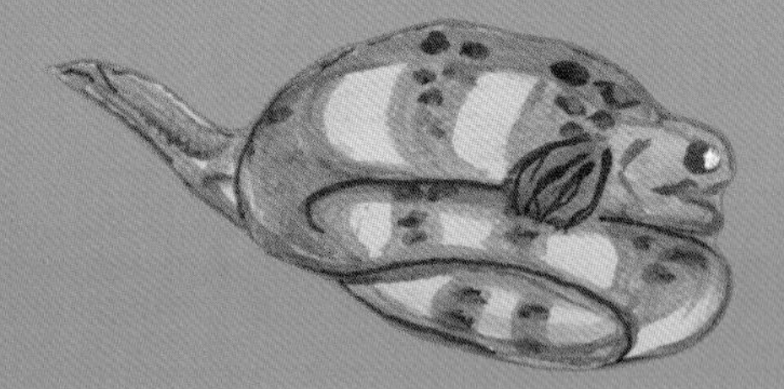

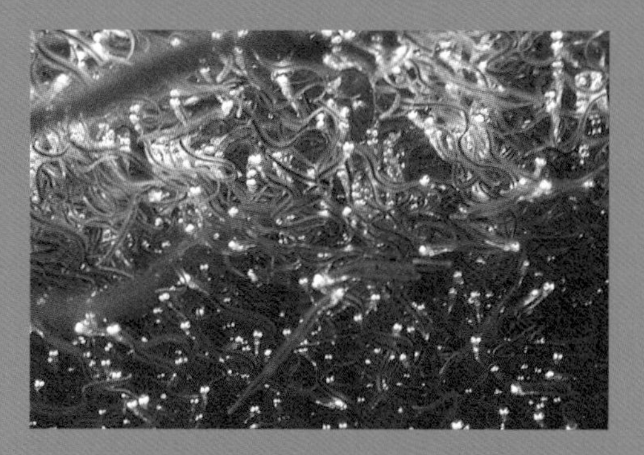

The Planktonic Larvae Stage

The baby Wolf-eels hatch at the same time as the spring plankton bloom so the babies have plenty of food.

The Pelagic Juvenile (free-swimming)

The Wolf-eels at this stage are up to six months old. They move around searching for food.

Benthic Juvenile (bottom-living)

At this stage the Wolf-eel is one to two years old. It will grow considerably. The Wolf-eel changes color to grey and develops the big canine and molar teeth it needs to crush crabs and sea urchins.

Acknowledgements

With thanks to
Dr. Jeffrey Marliave of
the Vancouver Aquarium Marine Science Centre
for his interest and advice.

With special thanks to
my husband, Rod, my life-long dive buddy.

Photo Credits

Back cover photos: clockwise from top left

Egg mass - © Dr. Jeffrey Marliave
Next two images of Wolf-eels - © Rod Stanley
Plumose Anenome - © Jacqueline Stanley
China Rockfish - © Doug Pemberton,
Octopus - © Jacqueline Stanley
Jacqueline scuba diving - © Rod Stanley

Portrait of Jacqueline - © Alvin Gee
Life cycle photos: clockwise from top center

First, second, and third - © Finn Larsen
Fourth - © Rod Stanley
Fifth - © Dr. Jeffrey Marliave

Editing by Suzanne Bastedo
Cover design by Jan Perrier and Sheila Henriques
Text design and layout by Sheila Henriques and Warren Denny

Published by Peanut Butter Publishing
Vancouver, BC

First Printing January 2000
Library of Congress Card Catalog Number 99-65378

Canadian Cataloguing in Publication Data
Jacqueline Vickery Stanley 1952 -
Wolfie the Wolf-eel

ISBN 0-89716-828-3

1. Wolf-eel--Juvenile literature. I. Title.
QL638.B6S72 1999 j597'.77 C99-910898-0

Peanut Butter Publishing

1656 Duranleau Street, Suite 212 Granville Island
Vancouver BC V6H 3S4 (604) 688-0320

Pier 55 Suite 301 1101 Alaskan Way Seattle
Washington 98101-2982 (206) 748-0345

Email: pnutpubv@axion.net
Internet: http://www.pbpublishing.com

The Adventures of an Undersea Creature

Written and Illustrated
by Jacqueline Vickery Stanley

1

2

It was a special day at the aquarium. Outside, the earth was starting to warm up after a long winter. The first crocuses and daffodils were popping up and new baby birds were chirping at their parents for food.

Inside the aquarium, hundreds of baby Wolf-eels were hatching. For over three months the mother and the father Wolf-eel had wrapped their bodies around the eggs. They had taken turns to protect and care for the eggs. When it was time for the eggs to hatch, the mother had fanned them with her long tail and gently squeezed them with her body.

Now the eggs had hatched. The baby Wolf-eels were very, very tiny. They looked a lot like tadpoles as they rushed around in their tank excitedly exploring their new home.

The young Wolf-eels were always hungry and they ate lots of very small fish and shrimps, which they especially liked. Very soon, they had grown so much, they were taken to a larger tank. This one had a glass wall and the Wolf-eels looked out at the strange creatures watching them.

"What are the creatures looking at?" one small Wolf-eel wondered out loud.

"US!" said another small voice nearby. "They are looking at us!"

The two little Wolf-eels looked at each other and saw a long bright orange body with very attractive brown bands and they could understand why the creatures outside their tank would want to look at them!

"What is your name?" asked one of the little Wolf-eels.

"William," the other replied. "What's yours?"

"Wolfie," he said. "Let's look for shrimp!" And they both rushed off.

Wolfie and William were the youngest of their very large family and they were the smallest so they tended to stick together. They spent their days eating and swimming and resting. They never tired of watching the creatures as they passed by the glass wall of the tank. Creatures who couldn't live in water — imagine!

The China Rockfish was an old resident of this tank. He enjoyed watching the young Wolf-eels wriggling and squirming in the water. He would often laugh at them rushing around in the tank. Wolfie and William followed the Rockfish around, but not too closely. The China Rockfish looked rather frightening with his black and yellow body and his sharp black dorsal fins which bristled when he spoke. Like all fish, the China Rockfish had dorsal fins along his back to help him swim and balance. He also used his dorsal fins to show if he was happy or angry. The China Rockfish usually looked angry.

To Wolfie and William, the China Rockfish seemed to know everything. One day, William bravely pushed Wolfie towards the Rockfish.

"Excuse us, Mr. Rockfish, my brother has a question," said William in his strongest voice.

The China Rockfish slowly turned around and glared at the young Wolf-eels.

"Why do you always laugh at us, sir?" Wolfie asked. His voice was very shaky. When the China Rockfish opened his mouth to speak, Wolfie was so scared that he jumped behind a small rock.

4

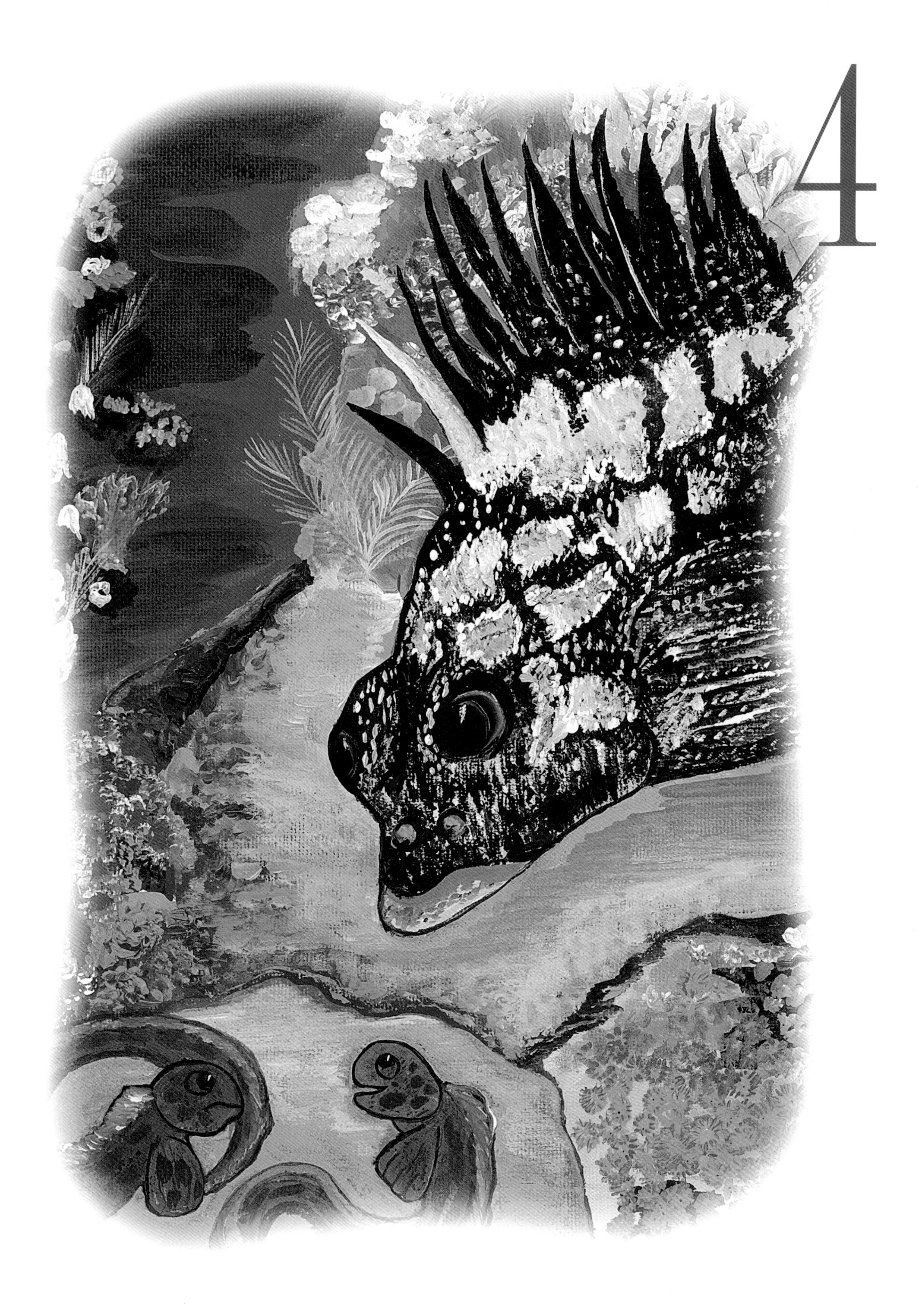

"Look at all of you," the China Rockfish chuckled, "wriggling and writhing and worming and squirming. You Wolf-eels are all mixed up! You act like eels but you are not eels!"

"We're not?" said Wolfie, peeking over the rock.

"What are we, then?" said William in a very worried voice.

"You are fish, a type called Blennies!" The China Rockfish sounded very clever.

"Fish?" said William.

"Blennies?" said Wolfie.

"Yes!" said the China Rockfish. He started to move away.

The China Rockfish was tired and had a very grumpy look on his face. But the Wolf-eels were very confused and very curious.

"Which are we, then?" they called after him. "Fish or Blennies?"

The China Rockfish looked even more cross. He stopped moving away and turned around to look at the two young Wolf-eels. He sighed.

"You are both. All of us creatures that swim in the sea are fish," he said. Then he quickly added, "Except for the mammals, of course. You are a special sort of fish called a Blenny."

"But you are a fish and we don't look like you," said Wolfie.

6

"Well, you can't help the way you look or the way you swim or that garish orange color, but you are fish!" The China Rockfish thought he had answered enough questions for one day. Then he heard a small voice.

"Well, if we are not eels why do they call us eels?" William asked.

"And why are we called Wolf-eels?" said Wolfie.

The China Rockfish swam towards the two young Wolf-eels. He looked at them very seriously and took a big breath.

"You are called eels because you look like eels on the outside. The wolf part of your name comes from your teeth. One day you will have huge teeth that look just like a wolf's teeth. Now, go away!"

Wolfie and William swam to the other side of the tank to get away from the China Rockfish. There they talked about what they had found out. They had no idea what teeth were yet or even what a wolf was, but the "huge" part sounded good. One day something about them was going to be huge!

Life in the tank was becoming a bit crowded as the Wolf-eels grew and grew. It was also becoming a bit dangerous. Wolfie and William remained good friends, but the other male Wolf-eels were fighting a lot. They were constantly bumping into the China Rockfish. He stayed mostly now in a quiet crevice between two rocks which happened to be just below where the Wolf-eels were fed. Any bits of food that the excited Wolf-eels missed drifted down to the China Rockfish.

7

One morning, the Wolf-eels were rushing around more than usual. They were being chased by a long net. Wolfie looked around quickly for his friend William.

William was gone! Wolfie couldn't see him anywhere. What was happening?

Very soon Wolfie was caught in the net. For a few minutes, he felt very heavy and strange as he was carried in the net. Then he was placed gently in cool water again. He swam away from the net as fast as he could. Then, he saw that he was in a new, bigger tank with bigger windows. Over by the biggest window, waiting for him was William!

"Phew!" they both said at the same time. "That was a close one. I thought I'd lost you!"

Then they laughed and laughed. The next time they saw the net they were not afraid because now they knew they were not going to be hurt. They were growing up, they were learning new things and they were changing.

In the new tank, the Wolf-eels began feeling bumps at the back of their jaws and they didn't rush around as they had when they were smaller. They also began to look different.

They were losing the bright orange bands and now they were turning grey. They became sleek and metallic-looking and very handsome.

The China Rockfish had not moved tanks with them. He had remained behind to teach the new young Wolf-eels and answer their questions. Wolfie and William remembered what he had said about their huge teeth. When the bumps in their mouths became big and hard, they smiled at each other, showing off their new teeth.

10

One day the Wolf-eels were taken from their tank again. This time they did not move to a bigger tank, but were plopped into a big barrel that was half-filled with water. The barrel was placed on a boat. The boat started to move. After a while, the Wolf-eels all felt sea-sick. They were bouncing up and down in their barrel as the boat bounced up and down over the waves.

Finally the boat stopped. The young Wolf-eels were all released into the cool water of the biggest tank they had ever seen. It was the Pacific Ocean.

Wolfie swam quickly away from the boat. How green the water was! He looked up and saw the sun shining far above the surface. If he had known what an emerald was, he would have thought that the sun shining through the water looked like a giant emerald.

Wolfie saw many other fish as he swam along. There were lots of China Rockfish, but none of them wanted to talk with him. He swam easily through the big branches of giant bull kelp and around stony ledges. He brushed by the billowy pillowy soft white plumose anemones that grew along a rocky wall. He swam down to a sandy patch where the sea urchins lived in big clumps. Wolfie didn't hesitate. He just knew that the urchins would be delicious. He took a huge mouthful from the sea urchin patch. Some of the spines poked through his cheeks.

If his mouth hadn't been so full he would have said to William: "So, THIS is what our teeth are for!"

But William wasn't there. In fact, now that Wolfie thought about it, he had been swimming alone for a very long time. Wolfie gulped. He realized that William had not been with him since he left the boat. But Wolfie knew this was something that he had to do by himself. This big, new place felt exactly right. Wolfie felt at home.

Suddenly, out of the corner of his eye, he spied a long tentacle with round suckers all along it. The tentacle came closer, feeling here and there as it moved across the bottom. Then Wolfie saw seven more tentacles attached to a huge body with eyes that looked as if they knew everything there was to know. Wolfie froze and stared. He had seen a Giant Pacific Octopus like this one at the aquarium. It was in another glass tank and it wasn't very big. At least it didn't seem very big. This one was gigantic! It was stretched across the sea floor. One tentacle was near Wolfie's half-chewed sea urchin. Wolfie couldn't see where the Giant Pacific Octopus ended.

12

Wolfie was thinking frantically, trying to decide what to do, when SWOOSH! Between Wolfie and the octopus a very fast creature zipped by. If Wolfie had hair, it would have blown over his eyes! The octopus and Wolfie looked in the direction that the creature had gone.

"What was THAT?" Wolfie completely forgot his fear and spoke out loud.

"That was a Steller sea lion," said the octopus. "They love to play."

No sooner had he said that when two more sea lions swam past. Wolfie thought they were beautiful creatures with their long, brown bodies and their powerful flippers.

One Steller sea lion threw Wolfie's half-eaten sea urchin to the other sea lion, who caught it and then threw it back. They continued to loop around, chasing each other at great speeds, changing direction in a moment, and barking at each other. Then they were gone.

Wolfie looked around. The octopus had gone too. What a place this huge, new tank was!

It was getting dark. Wolfie was tired. He swam slowly into the kelp, which settled around him like a blanket. But Wolfie liked to be deeper than the kelp, so he drifted down towards the rocky wall. He sighed happily when he found an opening in the ledge. He swam in and turned himself around so that he could rest as well as keep watch for the night.

"This place might not be so bad after all," he said with a yawn. "I hope William is O.K."

He began to doze.

All of a sudden a booming voice bellowed: "OUT!"

14

Wolfie was hurled out of the hole in the rock. Now he knew where the Giant Pacific Octopus had gone. Wolfie looked back and smiled his best smile. He hoped to convince the octopus to let him stay the night.

"Please, sir, just one night?"

There was no reply for a few moments. Then one long tentacle slowly snaked out of the den. After feeling and sniffing around the area, the tentacle collected two rocks and sealed up the hole so that no one could go in.

16

17

18

Wolfie sighed, then swam along the ledge, stopping when he thought he had found a hole for the night. Every time, he had to hurry away when he found someone already lived there.

Wolfie felt very tired. He was also starting to feel afraid. Suddenly he saw a familiar-looking fish. It was very big but it looked just like him.

"Hey! Hello! Are you a Wolf-eel?" he shouted, quivering with excitement.

The big male Wolf-eel turned slowly around and looked right at Wolfie.

Wolfie stared with his mouth open. The Wolf-eel had a massive head with great thick lips. Wolfie could see the huge teeth that the China Rockfish had told him about at the aquarium. Wolfie could see how he would look when he was full-grown.

Wolfie realized that the big Wolf-eel did not look happy to see him.

"This is MY den and MY family!" the big Wolf-eel said.

He roared so loudly that Wolfie felt as though the words were punching him. The big Wolf-eel lunged out at Wolfie. Wolfie jumped quickly but he still felt the sharp teeth grab his dorsal fin. Wolfie squirmed and twisted. Finally he was free from the Wolf-eel's strong jaw. He swam faster than he had ever swum before. He swam and swam and he did not even look behind him. He was afraid that looking would slow him down.

Finally Wolfie had to stop. He was too tired to swim any more. His heart was drumming in his chest. He felt hot and very weak and shaky and his dorsal fin was hurting. He fell to the sandy bottom and felt the kelp close around him. He didn't move or call to anyone. All he could do was lie very still. Soon he was fast asleep.

As Wolfie slept, the tide swept him between two islands. He was still sleeping when the tide changed and he was swept back again. The big ferries came past and blew their ship's whistles and still he didn't wake up.

Big logs floated back and forth with the same tide. Several seagulls were riding on the logs, resting and catching up on the news. They became very worried when they saw the young Wolf-eel being pushed around in the water.

Three Steller sea lions zoomed past. When Wolfie did not move, they turned back and circled him.

"Let's play catch with him!" they barked to each other. A sleeping Wolf-eel was a new kind of game for them.

Meanwhile, Wolfie was dreaming about how good it had felt to settle in that octopus den and how good the sea urchins had tasted. Just as he was dreaming about the biggest patch of sea urchins, he was flipped head over fins. As he banged into a bulky body, he woke up coughing.

FERRIES

"What's going on?" He tried to focus his eyes.

This is the most exciting place I have ever lived, he thought to himself. It just never gets boring at all! BUMP! He was hurled into another firm body and then again and again.

All of a sudden — silence. He swam a little and looked back. Nothing! Then, the sea lions were back, hanging upside down right in front of his face.

22

"What's going on?" he said again.

The sea lions laughed as they gracefully turned and flew past him. Then they stopped.

"You were sleeping for too long. You need to wake up and take care of yourself," said the smallest sea lion. She smiled at Wolfie with her big brown eyes.

"You need to find a den and a mate," said the middle sea lion.

"A mate?" said Wolfie.

"Yes," said the biggest sea lion. "You Wolf-eels always find a mate and you stay together for the rest of your lives. You Wolf-eels are so romantic." She smiled and hugged herself with her flippers.

Suddenly the smallest sea lion called out: "Divers!" The sea lions whisked away.

Wolfie followed the sea lions as fast as he could. Soon he saw some very strange creatures. He had seen them before at the aquarium and again on the boat. This was the first time he had seen them in the water. They were swimming, but not very gracefully, and they had lots of decorations. They had even more decorations on them than the Decorated Warbonnet Fish.

The Decorated Warbonnet Fish were so fond of accessories that their headgear often grew over their eyes.

These other strange creatures had not only strange headgear but also smooth, very odd-colored skin and very big eyes and two long fins at the end of their bodies. And Wolfie couldn't see any gills! How did they breathe?

Wolfie swam behind one of them and saw some strange objects on its back. Every now and then a huge cloud of bubbles would erupt from its mouth.

Wolfie went back with the sea lions and watched to see what these strange creatures would do. One of them picked up a sea urchin and broke it open, then held it out to Wolfie. Wolfie suddenly realized that he was simply starving. It had been ages since he had eaten. Without thinking, Wolfie swam over to the strange creature and took the sea urchin into his mouth. The orange roe, the eggs inside the sea urchin, were Wolfie's favorite food. Wolfie's big powerful teeth easily crushed the urchin shell and spikes. The strange creature gently stroked Wolfie's side and that felt very nice. Wolfie accepted another snack of sea urchin and then swam slowly away towards the rocky ledge.

24

Everywhere he looked, he saw sea urchins and wonderful swimming scallops. He carefully swam along the ledge, knocking softly at the entrance of any interesting holes. Before knocking, though, he checked for empty sea urchin or crab shells. If there were any shells at the entrance, Wolfie knew that an octopus might live there. An octopus was not fussy about where it left its garbage.

Eventually, Wolfie found a hole that he liked — and it had no garbage! Best of all, there was lots of food close by. What more could he ask?

For a long time Wolfie was happy in his home. It was just the right size and there were always plenty of sea urchins and swimming scallops to eat. Sometimes he even had a crab for dessert!

But one day Wolfie noticed that things were changing. The water was getting colder and the sun didn't shine down through the kelp as much as it had before. Winter was coming.

Wolfie had eaten all the sea urchins near his home and the swimming scallops had gone. He hadn't seen a crab for quite a while. It was time to move.

One morning he left his home. Wolfie worked his way down the rocky ledge with the tide. He moved into many new homes but each time he would run out of food. He kept swimming and looking.

After a very long time, Wolfie came to a new part of the ocean. He had never been there before. The walls were covered with big white plumose anemones and the kelp was thick. Wolfie swam down and found big patches of sea urchins. He was excited. I hope there is a hole for me, he thought to himself. Wolfie also remembered what the Steller sea lion had said about finding a den and a mate.

Underneath a rocky ledge, Wolfie found a big hole. He cleared his throat and was about to say something when a familiar-looking creature swam out of the hole. It was another Wolf-eel!

This time Wolfie was quick. Even though he was big now, he could still remember what happened the last time he saw another Wolf-eel. He swam and swam along the rocky ledge and through the kelp and anemones until he was sure he had escaped.

Finally, he looked back. He couldn't see anything. Wolfie slowed down for a moment to catch his breath.

"Wait, wait, please don't run away!" From behind him, he heard a voice calling.

The voice was soft but very strong. Wolfie thought the voice sounded wonderful. He waited to see who was calling but instead he saw the other Wolf-eel again. It was coming towards him very quickly. He sped away as fast as he could swim, but that same voice sounded even nearer. He looked to his right as he swam and to his left, trying to see who was calling. But first things first. He had to shake off that other Wolf-eel. Suddenly, he bumped into something. It was the other Wolf-eel!

"Wait, wait!" the Wolf-eel said between big breaths.

This was the voice! The wonderful voice! The other Wolf-eel swam next to Wolfie and then curled herself around him. This Wolf-eel was smaller than Wolfie and her face was far more elegant than his and she was strong and slender.

"Who are you?" Wolfie stammered. His voice sounded shaky and nervous.

"My name is Ella."

Wolfie stared and stared.

Finally he said, "I came from the aquarium and I have been by myself for a very long time."

Wolfie felt very sad while he told Ella what had happened to him since he had arrived in the ocean. Then he sort of felt himself being guided. He wasn't really swimming, and he realized Ella was guiding him back to her den.

28

Wolfie and Ella swam along the rocky ledge. Wolfie looked at Ella and felt very lucky to be with her. She was beautiful. But more than that, she was good to talk to and she was strong and smart. She was also very kind. Wolfie couldn't remember when he had felt so happy.

Soon they arrived at Ella's den and swam inside. Wolfie did not ever want to leave. He knew this was what he was meant to do. It was the same feeling as when he had swum away from the boat and felt so quickly at home, even though he never saw William again. Wolfie still thought about William, but he knew that if he needed to, he would fight William to protect his family. Now Wolfie understood the big Wolf-eel that had attacked him. Wolfie would do whatever he had to do to protect Ella and the family he knew they would have.

Wolfie smiled. He had found his place with Ella. Together they would live for many, many years and have many, many babies who would learn about life in the ocean.

o o o o o

30

It was a special day deep under the ocean. Wolfie and Ella's family had been growing fast. Now it was time for the young Wolf-eels to leave.

Wolfie smiled and sighed. The patch of sea urchins looked mouthwateringly delicious. He swam out of the den and took a huge mouthful, the spikes of the urchins sticking through his cheeks. He heard Ella's wonderful strong voice and he smiled again through his bulging cheeks.

"You young Wolf-eels should never try to take such a huge mouthful of food that you can't speak."

From inside the den, Ella was explaining to the small Wolf-eels important things that they needed to know before they left.

31

Wolfie swam back to the den and heard two small voices asking big questions.

"Well, if we are not eels why are we called eels?" said one.

"And why are we called Wolf-eels?" said the other.

The End

What Do You Know About Wolf-eels?

One thing that makes Wolf-eels so interesting is that no one knows everything about them!

1. How long does it take for a baby Wolf-eel to grow into an adult?

Wolf-eels go through four stages of growth. The first is when they are hatched. In the second stage, they become pelagic (or free-swimming). That means they do not live on the bottom or only in one place. In the third stage, they become benthic. Now they live only on the bottom. In the fourth stage, they remain in a den with one mate. They stay with that mate for life. Wolfie was about four years old when he reached the fourth stage.

2. How big do Wolf-eels grow?

Wolf-eels can grow from 1 to 2.5 meters (3 - 8 feet) long.

3. What do young Wolf-eels eat?

They eat soft-shelled foods such as herring, shrimp or crab larvae because young Wolf-eels only have pointy canine teeth at the front of their mouths. These teeth help the young Wolf-eels to catch their food but not to crush and grind it.

4. When do Wolf-eels grow their big back teeth?

Scientists think that when young Wolf-eels begin to lose their bright orange color and turn grey, they also begin to grow their big back molar teeth. The molars allow the Wolf-eels to crush and grind hard-shelled food such as sea urchins, scallops, snails and crabs.

5. How did Wolf-eels get their name?

The scientific (Latin) name for Wolf-eel is *Anarrhichthys ocellatus*, which means they are fish that swim like an eel. Their well-developed canine teeth resemble those of a wolf and give the Wolf-eel (the male in particular) a fierce-looking head. Wolf-eels belong to the Blenny family of fish.

6. Where do Wolf-eels live?

Wolf-eels are found in the seas from Alaska to Southern California. They like to live where there is food for them and where there are rocky areas with holes or crevices for dens. They can live in water as deep as 10 - 40 meters (30 - 120 feet).

7. Are Wolf-eels friendly?

Some Wolf-eels have become used to divers who bring food to them. Most Wolf-eels are shy around humans and might attack if they feel the need to defend themselves and their den. Wolf-eels can do serious harm with their powerful teeth.

8. Would Wolf-eels make good pets?

Wolf-eels would not make good pets because they need to have a lot of room and special, live food. You may never see a Wolf-eel in the ocean but you might see one in an aquarium.

9. How long do Wolf-eels live?

This is one thing that no one really knows. Maybe this is something that you could research and find an answer!

Order Form

Wolfie the Wolf–eel

Also available from your local bookstore

Canadian Funds		US Funds	
____ copies @ $23.95	$_____	____ copies @ $18.95	$_____
GST (7%)	$_____	Shipping: (1st book)	$ 4.00
Shipping: (1st book)	$ 6.00	Add $3: (for each additional book)	$_____
Add $4: (for each additional book)	$_____		
Total enclosed	$_____	Total enclosed	$_____

Make your check or money order payable to:
Elton–Wolf Publishing
We also accept VISA and Master Card

Name

Address

City, Province/State Postal/Zip Code

VISA / Master Card account number **Expiry date**

Phone (daytime) (home)

Elton–Wolf Publishing
Book Order Fulfillment Department
1225 Walnut Ridge Drive, Hartland, WI 53029 • 1-800-362-8832 ext 6043
e.mail <order@elton-wolf.com> • Web site <http://www.elton-wolf.com>

ISBN 0-89716-828-3
Printed in Korea